FREUD

THE PENULTIMATE BIOGRAPHY D. HARLAN WILSON

RAW DOG
SCREAMING
PRESS

Freud: The Penultimate Biography © 2014 by D. Harlan Wilson
ISBN: 978-1-935738-57-2
Library of Congress Control Number: 2013920630

First Paperback Edition, February 2014

Cover Design by Matthew Revert
www.MatthewRevert.com

Headliner No. 45 Font by Kevin Christopher
www.KCFonts.com

Raw Dog Screaming Press
Bowie, MD

www.RawDogScreaming.com

PRAISE FOR THE WORK OF D. HARLAN WILSON

"Provocative entertainment."
—*Booklist*

"A bludgeoning celluloid rush of language and ideas
served from an action-painter's bucket of fluorescent
spatter."
—Alan Moore

"New bursts of stream-of-cyberconsciousness prose."
—*Library Journal*

"Wilson writes with the crazed precision of a futuristic
war machine gone rogue."
—Lavie Tidhar

"Wacky experimental fiction."
—*Publishers Weekly*

"Fast, smart, funny."
—Kim Stanley Robinson

"Pomo cybertheory never tasted so good!"
—*American Book Review*

"Utterly original."
—Barry N. Malzberg

"If reality is a crutch, Wilson has thrown it away."
—*Rain Taxi*

For the Wolfman.

"His principal subject of complaint was that for him the world was hidden in a veil, or that he was cut off from the world by a veil. This veil was torn only at one moment—when, after an enema, the contents of the bowel left the intestinal canal; and he then felt well and normal again."

—Sigmund Freud, "From the History of an Infantile Neurosis"

CHAPTER 1

I walked into the dealer room of the biggest science fiction writing convention in the Anglophone world. Editors and publishers and writers and aspiring writers and over-enthusiastic readers stormed up and down the aisles and filled out the ranks. I noticed a few academics too. Bald and pensive-looking as half-dead frogs, they wore khaki shorts and long black knee socks and tried to stay clear of the fanboys.

"Holy hell I've never seen a bigger bunch of fuckin' dumbasses in my entire life."

I guess I said that aloud. Looming near the doorway like a Slender Man, the Master of Ceremonies asked me to leave. Next to him was the Guest of Honor and he

seconded the motion while straddling an excretion of speculative aficionados with his heavy legs.

I did a 90 minute workout in the hotel gym, then got drunk on Protein Freeze margaritas and left the convention. I wrote this biography of Sigmund Freud as fast as I could on the flight home.

CHAPTER 2

According to Wikipedia:

> The United States has the highest rate of obesity.
> Estimates have steadily increased, from 19.4% in
> 1997, to 24.5% in 2004, to 26.6% in 2007, to 33.8%
> (adults) and 17% (children) in 2008. In 2010,
> the CDC reported higher numbers once more,
> counting 35.7% of American adults as obese, and
> 17% of American children.

A thoroughbred European, Sigmund Freud wasn't obese.
In fact he was relatively trim and kind of a stringbean in
his elder years, preferring smoking to the overindulgence

of food. He took regular walks, but he didn't work out and his eating habits were in feverish need of improvement. Technically we can't fault him for this shortcoming. Nobody really knew about good diet back in those days.

Freud was a tireless workaholic. Neurotically so. But this is repetitious: all obsessions are empowered by the worm of neurosis.

Freud possessed a devout interest in numerology and believed he would die at the age of 61. He did the math and that's the number that tumbled out of the equation's chute.

Freud died at the age of 83. Mouth cancer. He had endured over 30 surgeries on his hard palate. He couldn't stop smoking cigars.

Das Ende.

CHAPTER 3

I know exactly what I'm going to do in this biography, unlike its predecessor, *Hitler: The Terminal Biography*, the first installment in my Angry Black Author trilogy, which took me awhile to figure out, a few minutes anyway, although I'm uncertain what to do in lieu of the "Exploding Airplane Chapters," a series of vignettes interspersed throughout *Hitler: The Terminal Biography* that focus on the avian exploits of a man named Alois Villafuerte. Let me begin by saying that, like some dictators, therapists and orators, I'm at my best when I'm telling other people they're at their worst. Without the riffraff I'm nothing.

CHAPTER 4

Here's a blurb I got for this biography from a fellow author (not a writer, an author). He's more successful than I am. Of course, I only solicit blurbs from authors that make more money and generate more acclaim than me.

> "Irrefutable proof that this author has mastered the literary smackdown."
>
> —Superior Author

His name isn't important. Blurbs don't sell books. That's a myth. I ask Superior Authors for them only to feed my ego. And yet when the authors give them to me I feel guilty and never read them again. Usually I don't even allow my

publisher to put them on or in the book. The prospect of somebody, especially a Superior Author, devoting even a fragment of their time to me turns my stomach. I'd rather forego the endorsement than have to withstand it.

CHAPTER 5

All of the motorcyclists have decided to wear their helmets even though the law doesn't require them to wear their helmets. It is at this moment that all of the motorcyclists crash and die.

The streets are quiet, desolate. You can hear a *solifugae* crawling across the dirt, its prickled legs cracking like brown thunder.

But this *réalité de la vie* is wildly insignificant. Consider a more pressing issue such as the physics professor who works at the University of Fostoria's Ludavico Campus. My campus. His frayed hair grows from the sides of his head like Arizona kelp and he's got a big swollen potbelly. It's as if he's following the potbelly, or the potbelly is stringing

him along. He works out with the best intentions, but he has no concept of weight training, and he lifts dumbbells and kettlebells and barbells as fast as he can, arms and legs moving like broken pistons. I often glance in his direction with an expression that says: SLOW THE FUCK DOWN ASSHOLE!!! I know he sees my expression. But he won't listen to it.

The physics professor shouldn't be working out at all aside from daily walks. He needs to go on a diet and get rid of his stomach first. Then he can think about lifting weights and so forth. We all have a core frame, but anybody can do anything with their body in terms of dropping fat and building muscle. Additionally, as I've noted before in other biographies, 90% of what you do with your body is contingent upon what you put inside of your body. Wake up and smell the potential of your germ cells.

The Ludavico Campus, where I am an Associate Professor of How to Tell the Truth, sits on a lake made toxic by all of the runoff from the farmlands that surround it. The physics professor lives on the other side of the lake and drives to and from work on a sputtering pontoon boat. He's nice enough, but I don't like talking to him. Here's our last conversation. I will begin the conversation *in medias res*:

". . . and he was, like, yeah, up there, that kite," I said.

"Kike?" said the physics prof.

"No. Kite." I thought about it for awhile. "Kike? Do people even use the word kike anymore?"

"White supremacists."

"White supremacists?" I thought about it for awhile. "Do white supremacists even exist anymore?"

"Yes. They all live in Coeur d'Alene, Idaho, the Nazi capital of America. They shave their heads and sit on their porches and stare at you when you drive by."

"When were you in Coeur d'Alene?"

"On my way to Spokane. My family lives in Spokane. I grew up there. There's a lot of white supremacists in Spokane too."

"Oh. All right." I thought about it for awhile. "Are you a white supremacist?"

He made a face. "No more than any other white man, I guess."

I will end the conversation *in medias res*.

CHAPTER 6

The idea behind this trilogy of biographies, which I referred to as the Angry Black Author trilogy in chapter 3 of *Freud: The Penultimate Biography* for the first time, is that it will achieve a parasitic connection with other biographies about Hitler, Freud, and whoever I'm going to write the final biography on (either Tom Cruise or Frederick Douglass) at Amazon.com, the only viable marketplace in the twenty-first century publishing world. Quality means less than nothing. What matters is who buys a book that sounds something like your book and then buys your book too. If somebody buys, say, *The Freud Reader*, which currently sells quite well at Amazon, and the same person buys *Freud: The Penultimate Biography*,

thinking it's similar to *The Freud Reader*, Amazon pools the titles together on its **Customers Who Bought This Item Also Bought** page and a snowball effect ensues. Because of this one sale, thousands of readers will now mistake *Freud: The Penultimate Biography* as a book that might be similar to *The Freud Reader*, even though, for sake of argument, they are really only linked by Freud's name in the titles. I've done this more than ten times with other books under different pseudonyms and it's worked like a charm: each pseudonym has become a bestselling author in a matter of weeks. Again, what's inside the book is altogether meaningless. For instance, in one of my alter-ego's books, each page contains a large black dot with this thick-skinned inscription:

THERE IS A HOLE HERE
WHERE SOMETHING ELSE USED TO BE

The depth of meaninglessness in this instance actually amplified book sales because readers, feeling cheated and hurt, wrote so many negative reviews. If there are enough reviews, it doesn't matter if they are positive or negative; as a general rule, the madder you make readers, the more they buy your bullshit, i.e., the more they allow and want you to take advantage of them.

THESIS: Quantity, as always, dictates desire.

CHAPTER 7

Already this seems less interesting than my Hitler biography if only in that Hitler was more famous than Freud and the stamp of his name on the cover of *Hitler: The Terminal Biography* will doubtless sell more books. But Freud was no slouch vis-à-vis celebrity culture. He more or less conjured psychoanalysis out of thin air (with a pointer or two from Jean-Martin Charcot), and he proved to have one of the most fervent and devoted work ethics on the planet—in his era, or any preceding or subsequent era. I dare you to find somebody with a work ethic stronger than Freud's. He went to the office all day and came home and read and wrote all night. He barely slept. When he wasn't working he got nervous; like so few writers, work

saved him from the flames of indolence. The many flaws of psychoanalysis are of little consequence. Psychoanalysis is useful and interesting in boundless critical and creative ways. Consider the broad scope of psychoanalytic literary theory alone.

Nonetheless the lack of Hitler in *Freud: The Penultimate Biography* produces a certain lumbering anxiety. A citation from William Shirer's *The Rise and Fall of the Third Reich* or John Toland's *Adolf Hitler: The Definitive Biography* may lift the spirits, but it could also temporarily derail the narrative from its current path. At the very least it will inhibit the narrative's velocity and cause it to decelerate. Freud will have to suffice.

Escaping from Germany to England in 1938, Freud was on the lam from Hitler when he died in 1939. Celebrity status aside, people tend to like to read about antagonists, about the evils human beings are capable of, more than protagonists or characters who spend all their time at the office and at home. As I hope to show, Freud was a bad guy in his own right.

To begin again, I want to share this passage from Anthony Storr's *Freud & Jung: A Dual Introduction*:

Most people of outstanding intellectual achievement exhibit traits of personality which psychiatrists label obsessional; that is, they are meticulous, scrupulous, accurate, reliable, honest, and much concerned with cleanliness, control and order. Only when these admirable traits become exaggerated do we speak of obsessional neurosis, a disorder which ranges in severity from mild

compulsions to check and re-check to a state of total disablement in which the sufferer's existence is so dominated by rituals that normal life becomes impossible.

As my students often say as a means of commentary and interpretation: "Well, that quote speaks for itself."

CHAPTER 8

A mechanic is fixing a car and it breaks down. This thing can't break down, it's already broke, he thinks to himself. He decides to call it a day.

He's tired but he goes to the gym anyway. He's a bodybuilder and the next competition is only one month from now. No excuses for slacking off.

On the way to the gym his car breaks down. He gets out to fix it and the car breaks down again and then while he's fixing it the thing breaks down again.

This can't be happening, he thinks to himself.

He starts to hitchhike to the gym but nobody picks him up and eventually his legs stop working. He falls down. He flails on the roadside like a broken insect. Somebody pulls

over to help him and gets out of their car and their legs stop working. Everybody's legs stop working. There's a lot of chaos and anxiety but after awhile everything goes back to normal. The mechanic's legs are working again and his car starts and he has a feeling that the car he was fixing back at the shop will let him fix it now. He drives to the gym without incident. He has a good workout and gets a good pump. Then he goes home and tucks his kids into bed, thinking to himself: What a powerful day . . .

CHAPTER 9

As I noted in *Hitler: The Terminal Biography*, the mind is the prison of the body and vice versa. Hence I exercise both facets of my character with equal rigor.

Context is everything.

Apropos.

I stepped too close to a disabled person in the locker room. He got mad at me. I don't know what was wrong with him, but his mouth looked more like a half-open zipper than a mouth, and his spine was crooked, and his ears didn't seem to belong on his head.

He antagonized me throughout my entire workout.

He followed me from station to station and he carica-tured the exercises I did while making loud groaning

and sucking noises. When I got on an elliptical machine, he stood in front of me and gawked and blubbered and hooted and swung his arms up and down and up and down, parodying my labors.

Afterwards, back in the locker room, he watched me get undressed and laughed like a hyena while I used the toilet and then took a shower. As I put on my clothes, he barked inarticulately at me, drool frothing and slobbering from the zipper. I think he was trying to tell me that I shouldn't have stepped so close to him . . .

Of course, in *Freud: The Penultimate Biography*, the story can only end in one way.

But how might the story have ended in *Hitler: The Terminal Biography*?

CHAPTER 10

During the flight, the chief executive of my publisher called me. He was frantic. There was a lot of white noise and I only heard the last part of his tender rant. It went:

> . . . and you are working in a different profession. You are an author. They are writers. Anybody can be a writer; you pick up a pen and write something. You may even get published. But that doesn't make you an author. An author is a writer by profession, and via the context of social strata a philosophical warrior influencing the development of critical thinking. It's like saying the Hulk is a bodybuilder. No: HE'S THE FUCKING

HULK. That's the difference between you and genre writers. And all writers.

I said, "That's going in my Freud biography. Now." I hung up the phone and typed it into the tenth chapter.

And then, minutes later, I got this blurb via text from a Superior Author who I'd solicited to endorse *Freud: The Penultimate Biography* a few minutes ago. Sometimes these things take awhile.

The blurb said, "You can't write unless you can write like the author of *Freud: The Penultimate Biography*."

Good blurb. I never used it.

CHAPTER II

John Landis's conclusion: "He just wanted do dress up, put on a mask, and growl like an animal. It's really as simple as that."

Landis directed *An American Werewolf in London*. The film's special effects set new cinematic precedents and received an Academy Award for Outstanding Achievement in Makeup. It caught the eye of Michael Jackson, who subsequently hunted down Landis to get him to direct the music video for *Thriller*, which also set new precedents in its respective artistic medium. The video is fourteen minutes long. In it Jackson sings and dances and turns into a wolfman.

Der Wolfsmann.

As is always the case when we hear the term, we immediately recollect Freud's seminal case study, "Aus der Geschichte einer infantilen Neurose" (trans. "From the History of an Infantile Neurosis)," and wonder how we might plug it into other outlets. At first we become excited by the prospect of the doctor psychoanalyzing a werewolf, but then we remember that Freud's Wolfman was not a lycanthropic changeling, and in fact Freud never called his Wolfman a Wolfman, and he never thought about his Wolfman as a Wolfman, a term retrospectively applied to the subject in question after Freud got famous.

The Wolfman's name was Sergei Pankejeff. He had a drinking problem.

Vodka.

He justified it by telling himself that all Russians drank too much vodka. True enough. What wasn't true was that Russians somehow developed the capacity to handle the Drink and live long, healthy lives. This is what Pankejeff told himself even as all of his family and friends died of cirrhosis and pancreatitis and Wernicke-Korsakoff syndrome. The fact is Russians are like Native Americans and can't handle their liquor, no matter what form it takes. Liquor is actually more aggressive and damaging to Russian corporeality than it is, say, to the corporeality of your average African-American and Irishman, both of whom possess organs and arteries cast in rustproof iron.

One night Pankejeff got drunk and went outside and saw a bunch of white wolves in a tree. Startled, he called the first person that leapt to mind.

Freud said he would be right over.

He took a plane and the plane exploded but not until it had landed and Freud was well out of range, waiting for his suitcase in baggage claim.

Pankejeff sent a cab to get him. Freud relished a long cigar on the ride over. He was as addicted to cigars as Pankejeff was to vodka and really whatever alcohol he could get his hands on. The main reason Freud didn't like flying was because he refused to smoke on planes. Airlines allowed it back then, but something about the altitude inhibited his psychosomatic pleasure, even though his body experienced a dire Need.

The cab pulled up to the estate. Freud got out and exclaimed, "Wolfman!" striding forward and extending his hand. He paused. "Wait we're not there yet. I mean I haven't heard your story yet and so you're not the Wolfman yet. I mean I'm not supposed to know your story yet and so forth. You're not a Wolfman. Forget about all that. Pardon me. Another cigar perhaps."

They retired to the study.

"So what's going on?" asked Freud, his beard concealed by a tawny cloud of smoke.

Pankejeff said, "I hear little girls screaming next door. Do you live next door?"

"No. I live down the street from my office. I have six children. Sometimes they scream. I don't think they're screaming now. But what do I know. They could be screaming or not screaming."

"It must be hard to work with all that screaming going on. Goodness gracious. I have some kids. They scream sometimes and I can barely handle it. That's why I drink too much. Well I guess I'm Russian too. Maybe what I'm

hearing right now is, like, residual trauma. Echoes of my children's screams."

"That could be. That could be."

"That reminds me. I need a drink."

"By all means."

Pankejeff poured himself a vodka and drank it. "Mm. That feels better." He poured himself another vodka and drank it. "Mm. That feels even better." He poured himself one more vodka. "God I like the way that tastes. Good lord. There's something about vodka, you know? Well I feel pretty good now."

"Good. I want you to feel comfortable."

"I do. Thank you. Thank you for coming too. I appreciate it."

"Not a problem."

"Anyway it's tough to think about things with all that screaming going on. I like to keep my place clean too, but when you have little kids running around screaming all the time, they mess everything up. All I do all day long is clean up and drink."

"I see. It sounds like you might have a spatial malady of sorts."

"I do. I need a clean space to work in."

"What kind of work do you do?"

Pankejeff looked around. "You know it just occurred to me that we're not in your office. We're at my house and that screaming I hear probably belongs to my children."

"Probably." Freud finished his cigar and put it out. "Well I think I have enough to go on for now."

Pankejeff fell down. He got up and said, "Really? But I need to tell you about my bowel movements. They're

horrible! And then when I was a kid I accidentally saw my parents having sex. They were doing it doggystyle. The primal scene. But that might have been two animals. I don't trust my memory. Then there's the walnut trees outside and the wolves in them. Those damned wolves. I might have had a dream about them being in the tree, but then again, I might have looked out the window and saw them for real. I think I called you because I had a dream. What does that mean?"

"Wolfman!" exclaimed Freud, leaping from his chair and lighting another cigar.

CHAPTER 12

Sound of Pac-Man's death. *La petite mort.*
Reboot.

CHAPTER 13

Somebody pulls over to the side of the road and puts the car in park. They don't turn the car off.

The car idles. The car

idles. The car idles. The car idles. The car idles. The car idles. The car idles. The car idles. The car idles.

"Damn this car," somebody says, putting it in neutral.

CHAPTER 14

A mechanic wishes he weren't a mechanic. He wishes he were a writer. Writers are smart and capable and make lots of money and lead fulfilling lives. They don't have to wash their hands with lava soap all the time either.

He writes a novel and goes to a writing convention.

First things first: the hotel fitness room. Then the mechanic runs the gamut.

He goes to the bar and does some networking.

He goes to a panel and asks a question.

He goes to his room and watches TV.

He looks out the window at the pool.

He goes back to the bar and does some more networking, shaking hands firmly, but only on the first pump.

He leaves the bar and ambles around the hotel and calls a few people names.

He goes back to his room. The TV won't work. He goes into the bathroom and looks in the mirror. He forgot to take his jumpsuit off.

This is your brain on reality, he thinks to himself.

He goes back to the bar and drinks too much and networks some more and shakes hands without discretion or invitation and yells at anybody who gets too close to him. He feels good. Lots of networking going on. People know who he is now. He's met agents and other writers and probably everything's going to work out for him.

CHAPTER 15

As evinced by the first installment in the Angry Black Author trilogy, *Hitler: The Terminal Biography*, I succeed like a virtuoso when I aspire to fail. As such, *Freud: The Penultimate Biography* will exhibit similar mettle and abide by my guiding mantra:

TRY LESS. WIN MORE.

That said, while my writing invites certain deployments of critical inquiry and odium—I mean the writing I've done that clearly bears the mark of TRYING TOO HARD—you can say nothing about my raging angle of incidence and above all the prowess of my prose. In business meetings

we call it "Hörnblowér prose." Derived from the name of the director of the Beastie Boys video "So What'cha Want," Nathaniel Hörnblowér, pseudonym and alter-ego of Beastie Boy MCA (a.k.a. Adam Yauch, RIP), this manner of prose, like the video, combines thermographic werewolf (à la *Wolfen*) and infrared hunter vision (à la *Predator*) points-of-view with a photo-negative effect and double-time image-making. A more accurate and genuine description might be "Earthfucker prose," a writing style that speaks for itself and is more or less without peer. The third and final installment in my scikungfi trilogy of novels, *The Kyoto Man*, is the archetype. Kissing cousins include the first two installments in my scikungfi trilogy, the splattershtick *Codename Prague* and the satirical *Dr. Identity*, both immodest instances of earthfucking in the narrative rye.

Here's the sixteenth chapter of my biography on Sigmund Freud:

CHAPTER 16

On self-publishing.

Maybe if you become a god it's all right. Otherwise YOU ARE NOT THAT GOOD. YOU NEVER WILL BE.

James Joyce and the fat woman with the dyed black hair—they're all fat women with dyed black hair—who wrote *50 Shades of Gray* filled too many dummies with hope. Of course, this is the nature of capitalism: to facilitate hope while always-already treading the waters of the Abyss. With some vintage exceptions, we are all Willy Lomans lying in wait for the quickfire Rise and the terminal Fall.

Then again, the publishing industry isn't what it used to be.

CHAPTER 17

Biographer is a slang term for autobiographer.

Facebook, Twitter, Goodreads, etc.—in the contemporary world, few writers can stay afloat and develop a readership without these social networks.

I don't use them and I don't believe in them.

My utopian perception of literature is patently Romantic. As William Blake writes in a passage from "The Human Abstract":

> And it bears the fruit of Deceit,
> Ruddy and sweet to eat;
> And the Raven his nest has made
> In its thickest shade.

The Gods of the earth and sea,
Sought thro' Nature to find this Tree,
But their search was all in vain:
There grows one in the Human Brain.

Blake's memorandum on the "nature" of intellect belies my intention to devote the rest of *Freud: The Penultimate Biography* to online culture and my experience therein. I would begin with the first time I contacted residents of Shanghai using a PASCAL program that an Indian student (Pranay Kumar) made for me in college because I was too lazy to do the work for class (Computer Programming?) and I paid him a case of beer (Natural Light) to help me. This was before the Internet proper. 1990 or so. Then I would discuss my first experiences with AOL and how I eventually turned to an academic web service and finally graduated to Yahoo, where I currently reside. About 15-20 years needs to be covered here. Many interesting things happened to me online during this period as I opened and closed documents, moved between websites, and waited for hours on the phone to talk to tech support about various issues.

Nevertheless I don't want to be your friend on Facebook and Goodreads and so forth and I don't want to follow you on Twitter and Instagram and so on. I (viz., my pseudonym) am your friend and follow you only insofar as it facilitates and energizes my authorial daemon. Don't post the following on my wall: "Great to connect with you. I hope you'll check out my latest novel. It's a great novel. Enjoy!" I don't care about your dumb fuckin' novel. I don't read fiction. I only read Lacan. I certainly don't

run my author pages for Facebook, Twitter, Goodreads, Flickr, Diaspora, Elftown, LinkNLog, Frühstückstreff, StumbleUpon, Plurk, LibraryThing, LiveJournal (Russian only), LAGbook, AbyssinianMaids, IFearTheeAndThyGlitteringEye!, S/Z, Evanrude, Flixster, JabFab, BlackPlanet and MotherfuckerBeware. Running my sites is what underachievers and proles and graduate students and homeless people are for. My subordinates have been given strict instructions re how to negotiate your friend-me terrorism. I can smell the desperation on your breath all the way from my subterranean home theater. Should you choose to make contact with me, you may expect to be blocked, deflected, and wiped from the face of my Arf. I tell you this only because I care about your wellbeing and I don't want anybody to get their feelings hurt.

Now let's talk about the moon.

CHAPTER 18

The government approached a famous movie director and asked if he would fake the moon landing for them.

"Fuck no."

The government approached the famous director again and encouraged him to fake that moon landing.

"Get the fuck outta here."

The government approached the famous director again and said c'mon really you should do this.

"All right fine," said the director. "I'll need some scotch-light screens and bean-splinters and some more fancy something-or-others. But I want to shoot it on the moon and I get to pick my own actors. For the lead, my gut instinct says Kirk Douglas, but my gut always tells me

to go with Kirk, capiche? Now that I've thought about it a little though I'm thinking, like, I don't know, Moses Gunn or something."

"Moses Gunn? What was he in?"

"He's black."

"Oh."

They took him to the moon. On the way there the director asked a government official why they wanted to fake a landing.

"We don't want the Russians to see what we're doing up there. We're doing things on the moon."

"I guess I don't care. That seems like a good reason I guess. There could be anything going on up there. Probably you're making pornos up there or something but what do I care. Some pornos are pretty good."

The director went to the East Bay with the actors and they all crammed into an EVA pod and he told them how they were going to shoot this damned thing. He could smell Moses Gunn's breath. The actor's skin smelled funny too.

"White people smell just as funny to us," Gunn noted.

The director said he knew that and decided there wasn't enough room, so they got out of the pod and just walked freely around the bay as the director told them what to expect in terms of blocking and all that and then he handed out the script.

There were some off-the-cuff rewrites. One of the actors didn't like how they were all supposed to bound across the surface of the moon like inflated air-monkeys. Other actors worried about lighting and more real-world issues such as the flow of oxygen into spacesuits. Gunn didn't care about anything as long as he got paid. With

a veteran's social finesse, the director attended to everybody's needs and they shot the footage and it all went pretty well.

The cameramen shot things in slow motion to convey a sense of low gravity even though in reality that wasn't how people would move on the moon; they'd move normal-like but with more featheriness and they'd go up and down and so forth. But people on earth expected moonwalkers to move in a certain slow-like way so that's how they shot it.

On the ride home the government official told the famous director it was a good thing he did that. Now he could go and make whatever kinds of movies he wanted, for the rest of his life, and the government wouldn't interfere or kill him.

"Do you really think you would have killed me? I don't think you would have."

The government official said well maybe not but we'll never know. Anyway that's some good moon footage you shot up there on the moon and we really appreciate it and so forth.

That night, after Vespers, the director went out for a drink with his wife. They sat at a table near the ocean and the moon loomed overhead like a death wish. Moonlight cascaded across the water from the horizon to the beach and seemed to spill into their wine glasses. They drank the most expensive bottle of pinot grigio the restaurant had to offer and then ordered another bottle plus two servings of sorbet.

CHAPTER 19

Later, while making love, the director's wife got a really bad feeling and rolled off of her husband. "Something horrible is going to happen," she said.

The phone rang and she closed her eyes and started to shake and pray.

The director answered it. "This is Donovan Ogg. Oh hello. Yes. Yes. Yes. No. Possibly. We'll have to see about that. Yes. Yep. All right well goodbye." He hung up.

"Who was that?" said Mrs. Ogg.

"The Secretary of State. I shot a short film on the moon today and apparently the spaceship blew up. Exploded, like. Everybody burned and died."

"Oh dear."

"Yeah they said whenever something flies it has to explode at some point because the laws of physics or physiques or something demands explosions and grief from objects and inhabitants of objects that think they can defy gravity without consequences."

"Oh dear."

"The funny thing is the ship blew up before we even landed on the moon and made the movie according to the Secretary of State so I really don't know what to think."

"Goodness me."

"Yeah I know but the thing is I feel fine so I'm going to assume I didn't explode with the rest of the crew and somehow this movie I made exists. I edited the footage on the way back to earth for Chrissakes. I think somebody's just having a little fun with me. It's ok I think. And if it's not ok it'll probably be ok at some point, for somebody, somewhere. I feel good."

They finished making love and reverted to the final paragraph of the last chapter sans the first sentence.

CHAPTER 20

Strange hexagonal patterns punctuate the motel. The resonance of their signification extends to the far shores of proto-consciousness. A regressed simian idly disagrees with the verdict. Soft primordial matter springs from the isolation tank. This conundrum originated in a university lab. And the didactic tempest—there's nothing worse than an intelligent storm. Cape Canaveral slouches into the Gulf like a creature that regrets being spit onto the beach and robbed of its gills. The benefits of sensory-deprivation are all that matter. *Banisteriopsis caapi*. An oceanic feeling of purpose and eternity flickers in the night. I am reminded of subliminal motorcades and radioactive mosquitoes starved for blood. Now we're getting somewhere.

CHAPTER 21

I spent years with Tibetan monks so that I could learn how to lower my pulse rate to zero and effectively stop my heart from beating. After awhile people thought I was dead and tried to bury me. Hence the expression: "Everybody's a gravedigger." The experience was as exhilarating as it was utterly pedestrian and inoperable. I told my therapist about it and in the next breath negated my pulse. My therapist yanked me off the chaise and got a shovel and tried to bury me. I left the building. Outside my father was waiting for me with a shovel and he tried to bury me too. I told Dad to take it easy and he reluctantly acquiesced, but he had already informed the neighbors of my demise, and they showed up with shovels and expected a funeral. So I

borrowed somebody's shovel and dug my own hole and got inside and pretended I was dead and everybody gathered around me and shoveled some dirt on me and prayed and paid homage. This experience lacked interpellation altogether. Almost everybody had nice things to say during the ceremony, and the ones that didn't say anything nice really made an effort to conceal their enmity. Afterwards I climbed out of the hole and took a shower and we had drinks and I even told the people who didn't like me that they could hang around for awhile. All you have to do with me is make an effort and I'll usually forgive you for your kindhearted animosities, your lukewarm aggressions.

CHAPTER 22

New character.

Name: John Vitruvian.

John Vitruvian uses porcelain chopsticks to eat sashimi over brown rice only until the wasabi runs out. And once the wasabi runs out, the sashimi and the rice cease to exist along with the chopsticks and the very musculature and identity of John Vitruvian himself.

CHAPTER 23

We planned my descent into drugs and alcohol carefully. I started by leaking a few choice photos to the local newspapers, then went global with extended video footage and finally a full-length IMAX reality movie chronicling three of my infamous "25 hour days." I didn't actually do any drugs. I took a lot of placebos that looked like drugs and they felt like drugs but they weren't drugs. Essentially I acted stoned and carried on. Instead of whiskey, I drank water with food coloring in it, etc. The whole sting went over really well and culminated when I chased down and stabbed a llama in Dubai during a parade. In America alone I probably sold upwards of one million copies of *Freud: The Penultimate Biography*. *Hitler: The Terminal*

Biography did even better. Afterwards I was tired and disappeared from the spotlight for months, working out and drinking protein shakes at my private gym on Maui near the Napili Kai beach resort where I vacationed with my family as a child. We'll do it again in a few years when there's a dip in book sales.

CHAPTER 24

I go through periods where I do several interviews in a single day and periods where I refuse to do them at all. Sometimes I want to talk about myself and sometimes I don't want to talk about anything. Freud experienced similar oscillations of desire—one moment the extension of his selfhood into the social matrix seemed imperative, if not compulsory; the next moment it appalled him. Here's an abridged transcript of an interview I did with Freud when neither of us were in the mood.

> **Freud:** I enjoyed *Hitler: The Terminal Biography*. You know a lot about Hitler. How many years did you spend researching the project?

Biographer: *Hitler: The Terminal Biography* isn't about Hitler. It's about me. Specifically, it's about my experiences as a person.

Self-conscious, Freud tensed the muscles of his face and studied the grooves in his skin.

Biographer: You didn't read it, did you.

Freud: I read the first sentence.

Biographer: No you didn't. If you read the first sentence you'd know what you're talking about.

CHAPTER 25

Freud was at the zoo and said, "That primate frightens me." And everything became clear.

According to Wikipedia, "The uncanny (Ger. *Das Unheimliche*—'the opposite of what is familiar') is a Freudian concept of an instance where something can be familiar, yet simultaneously foreign, resulting in a feeling of the thing being uncomfortably strange or uncomfortably familiar. Because the uncanny is familiar, yet strange, it often creates cognitive dissonance within the experiencing subject due to the paradoxical nature of being attracted to, yet repulsed by, an object at the same time. This cognitive dissonance often leads to an outright rejection of the object, as one would rather reject than rationalize."

Freud was talking mainly about inanimate objects, such as a house with two windows and a door on the front, the overall façade of which, when you look at it, seems to possess human qualities, like a human face and so forth. But his reaction to the monkey at the zoo produced an adverse effect: a living organism that in its livingness created a sense of the uncanny.

Have you ever seen a monkey at the zoo? Like, an orangutan? They're huge. They have hairy legs and hairy arms and sad, hairy faces. They don't want to be there. They want to be in a real jungle, not an interned simulation. They know the difference. They look like empty nests. The kids ogle them and the kids love it, but the orangutans all want to kill themselves. They just don't know how to do it. They don't know what that feeling means. That's what separates the orangutans from the humans. That's the only thing that separates us. The capacity for suicide. An orangutan will loaf and swing in a cage for years and despite its unhappiness will keep on loafing and swinging. Freud realized this dynamic with terrific clarity and it devastated him. The orangutan as the uncanny. What would it do to his theory of the uncanny?

I bought him a snowcone and a bag of peanuts on the way out of the zoo and that seemed to lighten his spirits, although he fell asleep on the ride home and had bad dreams. But he woke up feeling refreshed.

CHAPTER 26

A good magician's repertoire is only good insofar as he can operate the machinery of deflection and manipulate the cultural register.

Apropos.

On the next page are six viable titles for novels or memoirs appropriated from "The Egg Man," a song written and recorded by the Appalachian folk band The Egg Men. The lyrics preface my novel *Blankety Blank: A Memoir of Vulgaria*. The book isn't a memoir at all, despite the subtitle, although all of my novels are actually fluid memoirs, and so the subtitle, hanging there like a woebegone telltale, is in fact the very marker of truth that it appears, at first glance, to destabilize and subvert.

Apocalypse of Petroleum Sunsets
The Green Margarita
Flimflam Wastelands
Hell Yeah Baby
Egg Men, Igloo Kitchens and Mushroom Omelets
Crack of Love

We might push the latter two titles together and construct a work of critical theory with the last title functioning as the primary title and the second-to-last title functioning as the subtitle. Ergo: *Crack of Love: Egg Men, Igloo Kitchens and Mushroom Omelets*. Whatever the case, these titles speak volumes and render the books themselves utterly superfluous. One need not read them, let alone write them.

CHAPTER 27

It took me awhile to get back into MandrillCon.

They really didn't want me there and that's why the book's gone on so long with only the one reference to MandrillCon (sans name) in the first chapter. Technically this biography started writing itself, though, so I told the pilot to turn the plane around and he flew me back to Ohio, home of virtually every SF convention in the science fictionalized world.

I walked around the hotel searching for party suites. Whenever I found one, I slipped inside the room and ate as much food as I could within the confines of my macros. I also drank any alcohol within reach, talking shit about horror writers more than anybody as I became drunker

and louder. They're the worst of any genre. The least literary and the least style-oriented and the least educated. They all wish they were H.P. Lovecraft. They don't understand that Lovecraft was really just a Klansman with an underbite. And horror publishers and editors don't know what a typo is. But they're run by people—men, almost invariably—who perceive themselves as intelligent and supercool and in possession of interminable registers of sex appeal. Let me assure you: you've never seen a human being with less sex appeal than a horror publisher, or a horror editor, or a horror writer.

I spoke the Truth aloud.

There was a chase and I ended up in another room eating hummus and drinking shitty whiskey and leftover red wine (shiraz?). I spoke the Truth aloud again and there was another chase. Two chases later I was sanctimoniously drunk and got mad. I stopped dead in my tracks and turned around and tore off my shirt and started chasing the convention organizers who had been chasing me. I caught a few of them and punched and kicked and screamed at them until they calmed down and then I was alone in front of the hotel smoking a cigarette and watching gnats dance around a fluorescent light like rogue zygotes.

Dispossessed, I got in my Mini Cooper and drove it into the hotel.

I'm six-and-a-half feet tall. A man of that stature looks funny in a car that small, but there's more room than you think on the inside, and frankly I've never had a more comfortable driving experience.

I had no intention of running anybody over. I just wanted to scare people and do some fishtailing on the

carpet and so forth. I accidentally ran over a writer I didn't like, though, and I didn't feel too badly about it, so I started running over other writers and whoever got in my way as I raced up and down the hallways. I even made it up a flight of stairs once. Then the cops showed up and all that.

CHAPTER 28

Without question, Papyrus font is an insignia of low-grade sportsmanship; writers who, for instance, use it for the titles on the covers of their self-published novels call attention to their amateur status like the shriek of a fat woman during a church sermon. For all of their short-comings, big publishers wouldn't breathe the same air as Papyrus font. Nor would many small and mid-list presses. Years ago Papyrus was new and had a niche, but its time is over. Now it's not even fit to use on the menus of cheap Mediterranean restaurants or the glass doors of chintzy hair salons. Since the rise of variable computer typefaces in the 1980s, the font trade has become increasingly diverse and voluminous; there are infinities of more distinctive

hallmarks of authority. I was going to put the title of this chapter in Papyrus font to give you an idea about what I mean, but the probable embarrassment that would result precludes such a stylistic insurrection. And I feel like I would betray the clearly superior font (Top Secret) I have been using throughout *Freud: The Penultimate Biography* and that appears in the book's antecedent *Hitler: The Terminal Biography*.

CHAPTER 29

The ego as defense (*Verteididung*), as refusal (*Ablehnung*).
As disavowal. Understand this and you will understand
everything that emanates from my Bad Chi.

Also: love as hygiene.

CHAPTER 30

My daughter Maddie's goldfish dies. It's a blue goldfish.

"It's sleeping!" She pets the floating corpse.

Maddie's only five and my wife and I don't think she's ready for the death conversation, so I go to the store to get a replacement. There aren't any blue goldfish but I find a male beta. It's a deeper shade of blue than the old one. I'm confident I can spin the change of color.

I go to pay for it and the cashier asks for my ID. It might be a boy or a girl. There's a kind of mustache but like I said it might be a boy or a girl.

I looked at the cashier. "My ID?"

"You can make meth out of a fish, you know, if you grind it into a fine powder and combine it with Alka-Seltzer.

Some users snort the fish whole. That's called a World-builder. The act of snorting, I mean. The effects vary from user to user and some users don't feel anything other than mild sinus congestion," he said.

It was a boy.

My phone rang. I keep my volume on high and use a ringtone that's a recording of myself yelling as loud as I can. The cashier covered his ears. Most people do.

"Hello?" I said. "Hello? Hello? Hello? Is anybody there? Hello?" I heard wind or something. A harsh grating or something. "Hello? Hello? Hello? Hello? Hello? Is anybody there? Hello? Are you there? Hello? Anybody? Hello?" Somebody might have been talking on the other end but I couldn't make it out. "Hello? Hello? Hello? Hello? Hello? Hello? Hello? Hello? Hello? Hello? Hello?" I looked at my phone and somebody was still on the line. "Hello? Hello? Are you there? Is anybody there? Hello? Is anybody there? Is anybody there? Hello? Hello? Hello? Hello?" I looked at my phone and the number wasn't familiar. "Hello? Hello? Hello? Hello? Hello? Hello? Hello? Are you there? Hello? Hello? Hello? Hello? Hello? Hello? Anybody? Are you there? Hello? Hello? Are you there? Are you there? Are you there? Hello? Hello? Hello? Hello? Hello? Hello? Hello? Hello? Hello? Hello? Hello? Hello? Hello? Hello? Hello? Hello? Hello? Anybody there?"

I hung up and gave my ID to the cashier. The things I do for my kid.

CHAPTER 31

In the next chapter I want to continue to use the streetwise anaphora I so egregiously capitalized on in the last chapter. Then I'll refinance my angle of incidence.

CHAPTER 32

Somebody came up to me.

I waved them off and said, "I'm not interested."

They kept coming and tried to say something.

I spread my fingers and pressed my hand against an invisible pane of glass. Then I delivered this monologue:

"I'm not interested. Really. I'm not interested. Not interested. I'm not. I have no interest in you. None. I'm not interested. I don't care what you have to say. It won't interest me. I guarantee it. Really. It will not interest me. I won't find what you have to say to me interesting. Not even remotely. I'm really very extremely profoundly not interested. Nothing can make me interested. Because I'm not interested. It's not going to happen. Ever. Me being

interested, I mean. Do you understand? I'm not interested. I'm not interested. I'm not interested. No hard feelings. If it makes you feel better, I'm not interested in anybody. Well. I wish you luck placing the extension of your selfhood via oral transmission elsewhere. Somebody's bound to be interested in you. Somebody's bound to be. Somebody other than me. But I'm not interested. I'm just going to sit here for now. So if you could just, like, turn around and go away, that'd be great. Yeah. If you could turn around. Turn around. That's it. Turn around and go away. Turn around. Go away. That's it. That's it. That's it. So long. Thank you. Thanks. I'll be here all weekend. All right bye."

(NOTE: You may apply the above monologue to virtually anybody. Writer, car salesman, monkey trainer, monkey, certain Presidents of the United States—it's appropriate for multiple would-be interlocutors.)

Shortly thereafter I left the hotel bar and went to the lobby and got a program from the registration booth. The program was cheap-looking and poorly folded, but it had all of the information on it.

The awards ceremony was scheduled to begin at 6 p.m. sharp. Judging by the number of drinks I had drank, it was about 6 p.m. now.

CHAPTER 33

Abjected, I introduced myself to the Guest of Honor as Donovan Ogg.

"The famous director?"

I told him yeah and pretended I liked his books—never read his books; didn't even know who this guy was—and when he became disinterested and started to look through me I sort of leaned to one side and punched him as hard as I could in the kidney. He doubled-over and I punched him in the back of the head and he went down like a bag of slime. He had such a fat, weak neck, I thought I killed the GOH, but he was still breathing. He was supposed to give a speech in a few minutes.

I exited the dressing room.

There may have been some confusion had I not stuffed towels into my shirt and put on a fake beard and a dumb-looking fez and made myself into the biggest slob imaginable. It wasn't easy. I guess it worked, though, because I lurched onstage and limped over to the mic and nobody knew the difference.

"Good evening," I croaked. "It is very nice to see you all again. Tonight I want to talk about the creeping existence of writers and publishers and a lot of readers too. You fuckin' weirdos were a buncha creepy motherfuckers when you were teenagers and you grew up into a buncha creepy, stupid motherfuckers." I took a sip of water. "It's not entirely your fault. You took solace in escapist fanzines and Fletcher Hanks comics in order to negotiate the bullies that picked on you and beat you up because of how nerdy, weak, and insecure you were. More importantly, you never learned the importance of proper nutrition and exercise, above all weight lifting. 'Why should I lift weights?' you told yourselves, and still tell yourselves. 'My mind is what counts. I'm going to learn things and one day I will become so smart that those bullies won't matter anymore; their blows will bounce off of my brain tissue like a rain of baseballs bouncing off of a dirigible.' That's what you say." I took a sip of water. "The thing is, you're not so smart after all, and you really need to stop eating so much processed food. Everything you put in your mouth is processed! Meatball sandwiches and pizza and French fries and butter-based pastas and fried chicken and mozzarella sticks and sausage gravy and so forth. Not to mention all of the desserts. Forget about desserts. They're dangerously superfluous. Yes, key lime

pie contains protein because of the egg whites, but there's far more pollutants than nutrients in there. Get it out of your heads. Then, by extension, keep it out of your bodies. Point of fact: a good physique can't be sustained in the absence of a strong mind." I took the water and threw it at somebody. "Stick to whole foods you goddamn dummies! Also, work out with dumbbells. Use low weight at first. I'm talking, like, two-and-a-half to five pound dumbbells. That's less than most American pizzas weigh. Good lord!" I took off my hat and yanked off my beard and tore off my shirt. Towels leapt into the crowd like broken clocksprings. Animé-eyed, I reverently looked down at my abdominal rumblestrips, with deliberate slowness, as if saluting a dead soldier, then delivered a nearly incapacitating crowd-stare to the audience. "Yes. These are real. You're goddamn right they're real." I punched myself in the stomach as hard as I could. Unlike the GOH, I didn't flinch. "These abs are the product of years of continued hard work in my home gym. Yesterday I did 20,000 crunches. TWENTY THOUSAND!!! That was in one sitting, one set, without a break. I paused at the top of each crunch and flexed my abs to maximize results. And I was hanging upside-down, by my knees, on a crowbar that I jammed into the drywall like a javelin. It took me about six-and-a-half hours. Why did I do this? Because I am Goliath and when David flung that stone at me I caught it and ran over to David and I took that stone and BASHED HIS FUCKING HEAD IN!!! That's why, people. Hard work, people. And the desire to be different, unique, innovative, singular, revolu-tionary, pioneering, superheroic, super-egoic, omnip-otent, algorithmic, post-Zarathustran, and free. I hope

you all can hear me when I say that I am an Electromagnetic Earthfucker. I don't want to have anything to do with anybody who isn't. Good evening."

As I left the stage, a few spectators clapped, but overall everybody was kind of mad. As always, nobody's interested in the epistemological fruits of my Ph.D. in How to Tell the Truth.

CHAPTER 34

"When I kill my actors in a film," said Donovan Ogg, "I kill them in real life too. So it goes. Is that going to be a problem for anybody?"

The actors shook their heads.

"All right good. Now in this first scene everybody dies and the rest of the film is just aerial shots of Antarctica and the Orkney Islands and shit like that. Sound good?"

The actors nodded their heads.

"All right well I'm just going to kill all of you first and then figure out this first scene. It'll be easier for me that way. The easier things are for me, the easier things are for humanity. Capiche? Don't take it personally. It's just business. It's just art."

The second assistant director brought him a gun and he started to shoot the actors.

"You can't do that!" said Anna Freud. She had been hired by management to rewrite the script but she was late. Only minutes ago did she arrive on set and she wasn't even sure it was the right one.

"Who the fuck are you?"

The second assistant director leaned in and delicately informed Ogg that it was Sigmund Freud's daughter.

"Oh pardon me I'm really sorry. Boy oh boy Doc Freud's daughter. Things have been crazy today. Ok what would you do then? Should we wait to kill the actors until after the shoot or what?"

She didn't know. She had cried out on impulse as a coping mechanism; the violence was too close and too real for her to bear. She wondered what Father would do . . .

CHAPTER 35

Billy Idol's "Eyes without a Face" will be on MTV in minutes. I need to find a blank videocassette and load it into the VCR. Excuse me for a moment. I'm back. For whatever reason my agent signed me up to write and star in the Broadway version of Billy Idol's life. I will have to wear whiteface of course and dye my hair platinum but so would just about anybody. My publisher isn't happy about this project because they're not involved in it and won't receive any proceeds and they worry about me falling into the orchestra pit or something and getting hurt. Here's the video. Just a second. I need to hit the record button. There. I assured my publisher that I'm in better shape than most of mankind despite being over 40-years-old. 4% bodyfat and

deltoids like cannonballs and so forth. I also told them that I wouldn't drink during performances or even rehearsals as long as ample supplies of beta-blockers and several varieties of benzos (preferably lorazepam and oxazepam) were made available to me. This is a good video. I forgot how good it is. Idol commanded MTV in the 1980s along with Michael Jackson and Rod Stewart and a few other skinny short people. I must have seen this video 500 times and none of it seems familiar to me now. I like Billy Idol's hair. I wish I could do that with my hair. I can't say I dislike his singing voice either even though he clearly can't carry a tune. He's got nice white teeth. This video was shot in an era before over-the-counter teeth whitening technologies. Mind you. The hairdos of his background singers are yellow and stiff and long and look frozen in a timeless windstorm. Idol exudes a cool anger. There's fog everywhere. Clearly dispensed from fog machines. His favorite dance move appears to be holding a clenched fist near his face and flexing the arm. Now I know what to do. There's a lot to be said for mimesis. It informs our identities on and off the stage of life. Now an agglomeration of white women in tight black S&M outfits are slapping their backsides. I can't say I dislike this. Now Idol has entered a ring of fire and is surrounded by a taskforce of men in black cloaks and hoods. Possibly the KKK. Possibly a deviant sect of Trappist monks. I expect to hear a Gregorian chant at any moment. I didn't hear the chant. I have to go to the bathroom. I'll hold it. Well maybe I'll go. I'm back. I don't know if this video is supposed to be religious or racist. Perhaps neither. Or both. I need another drink. Thank you. I'm going to the gas station for more cigarettes. I'm

back. Things have calmed down in the video. Billy Idol has taken his shirt off and sprayed what looks like shaving cream all over his chest. He's still holding up his fist. Did I mention the snarl of his lips? Common knowledge. The video's over. I need to hit the stop button on the VCR. There. Well I'm more or less ready for the show.

CHAPTER 36

A unit of insufficiency and insolvency (viz., a writer) said, "There needs to be more literary rockstars. They don't exist anymore. Where have all the Ernest Hemingways and the Hunter S. Thompsons gone?"

"Hemingway?"

Long pause. Then:

"Hemingway was a whiny bleep. Have you ever read one of his novels? He's used the word 'pretty' in the last sentence of one of them. They're all about big whining bleeps who can't get what they want. Hunter S. Thompson wasn't all that different. He was just more sarcastic. And Thompson's druglust? And gunlust? Guns are for boy scouts and drugs are for big whining bleeps. How many

hours a day do you think these bozos worked out? The legacy of their fitness is deceptive. They have a reputation for being tough guys, hardbodies even, but I assure you, if you pressed a fingertip against their flesh, the imprint of your friction ridges would linger."

CHAPTER 37

Ernest Hemingway drank the rest of the wine and went to Germany and broke into Sigmund Freud's office. He retched on the floor and passed out on the chaise and was still there when Dr. Freud arrived in the morning. Dr. Freud told his secretary to clean up the mess and spray his office with potpourri and light a few candles and a stick of incense. When Hemingway woke up and got his bearings he apologized and told the famous psychoanalyst he didn't remember why he wanted to see him but it seemed important at the time. Dr. Freud said not to worry about it because the engines of desire are constantly whirring and revving and overheating and the worst thing Hemingway could do was feel guilty about just wanting to feel better.

CHAPTER 38

When I get drunk I usually take my shirt off.

I took my shirt off.

"Jesus Christ!" somebody said.

I looked down at my chest and abdomen. "I know. I haven't worked out yet today."

"No, I mean, you're, like, chiseled from stone," they said, dumbfounded.

"Let's say chiseled from onyx. Avoid clichéd expressions. But you should see me on Fridays. I carb-load on Sunday nights and it's only Monday."

I got a bottle of Smartwater from the minifridge and put my shirt back on.

CHAPTER 39

Now I think *Freud: The Penultimate Biography* is better than *Hitler: The Terminal Biography* despite Freud being less famous than Hitler. I was worried for awhile. A certain *déshabillée* continues to mediate my interzones but of course the geometry of my assertion and deployment depends upon it and I remain confident that failure is the only option.

CHAPTER 40

I forgot about John Vitruvian. Let's pretend he's Me for a moment. Too much actual Me can be a bad thing.

John Vitruvian only did interviews if the Dick Cavetts agreed to ask no more than three questions. Any more than three questions and he beat them up. He got arrested the first few times this happened but then the police sort of got used to it and readers and viewers started to like it. Now all of the Dick Cavetts are scared and only ask three questions. People don't like it.

Dick Cavett: Why do you hate writers so much?

John Vitruvian: I don't hate anybody. But I hate

slaves. And a writer ain't nothing but a cotton-pickin' slave.

Dick Cavett: What do you have to do to be a good genre fiction writer?

John Vitruvian: In order to write genre science fiction, you have to think up a good novum and push science to the outer limits of believability, bullshitting like an astrophysical maestro. In order to write genre horror, you have to be a really bad fucking writer and a dummy and perform various acts of violence on the body. In order to write genre fantasy, you have to read the *Lord of the Rings* trilogy and plagiarize it just enough so that you don't get caught and nobody sues you; also add more sex. In order to write genre romance, you have to be a fat woman with dyed black hair and own a bunch of mangy cats. In order to write genre detective and crime fiction, you need to memorize Edgar Allan Poe's "The Purloined Letter" and you have to live on a ranch somewhere in northern Michigan and do most of your writing in a souped-up shed. In order to write literary fiction, you need to use figurative language, include metanarrational footnotes, and try to be too impressive and clever. That's all of them more or less.

Dick Cavett: You are very muscular. My goodness. How did you get so big?

John Vitruvian: Pumping iron. Eating. There's nothing else to do in the pen.

CHAPTER 41

The way you block the body. The *savoir-faire* with which you articulate the limbs, the eyes, the physiognomic nodes and cavities—the armor of the Ego.

The best practitioners not only reify verisimilitude but negate the process of reification while calling attention to the seraphic arcology of the Self.

A writer, however, is under the assumption that s/he can perform onstage with a certain pizzazz that in fact reveals itself to the half-awake spectator as Dollar Store cant. Hence the Beckettian absurdity of the writer.

The mental fortitude of a professional showperson is monstrously underrated. Do you know what kind of focus a movie star has to have? Do you know how much

confidence a real author has to exert? And to control that confidence. And to maintain and regulate the focus. It's virtually impossible. In fact the persona doesn't exist. And yet there it is. All over the screen. All over the page.

Donovan Ogg tried to teach this paradoxical aspect of Superior Existence to a consignment of students. Once a year his philanthropic impulses get the best of him and he teaches an adjunct class in film studies at the University of Fostoria's Ludavico Campus. $80,000 per seminar.

"Well the first thing you need to remember is not to preoccupy yourself with isthmuses," intoned Ogg. "This is a problem a lot of people have and especially writers. Also don't spend time with potheads and other malcontents and definitely people who don't work out at least five days a week for 60-120 minutes per session. I mean, you want to have a good pump at least half of the time you're awake every day. Supplement your workouts with yoga and tai chi when you can and also only drink the good vodka. Belvedere. Grey Goose. That stuff in the crystal skull. The good stuff. I don't want to hear, like, 'I don't have any money and I can only afford Smirnoff or Sobieski or Svedka or even Skyy.' You need to spend money to make money. Holy Christ people you got to eat vegetables! Green vegetables. Eat them with every meal. Don't cook them. Cooking vegetables is for the Meek. Eat the vegetables raw and cook your goddamn meat. Is everybody really this fat and addicted to food? Look, don't read. It'll make you stupider. Watch every movie I have ever made and then watch them all again. The radiant Image, not the hollow Word, is what counts. This is valuable advice. You've already learned so much today. The world is nothing less

than a mineshaft of knowledge waiting for you to climb down to the pyrite at the bottom. Pyrite is what they call 'fool's gold.' It isn't worth anything. Therein lies the rub. I once took an elevator into a pyrite mine. I was a boy scout and went with my troop. We must have gone down more than fifty floors. It was fun. I remember the smell, but I can't put it into words. I won't put it into words. Words are for writers. I am a director. I am an actor. I am an artist. I am an author. Questions?"

CHAPTER 42

Time again for a coital interlude.

To my knowledge, there has not yet been such an interlude in spite of the claims made by the editor who wrote the cover description for *Freud: The Penultimate Biography*.

Coitus make me nervous.

It has to do with Christian guilt.

J.G. Ballard reminds us that coitus can be a powerful method of social change and revolution, yet we continue to repress coitality despite the maelstrom of porn that defines our daily lives.

I am among the Exposed Embryos.

History is the center of everybody's gravity and it can be difficult to arbitrate the circuitry of history in our

psyches, all of which are constantly revised by cultural productions and elocutions.

But I understand that mankind enjoys coitus and sometimes readers read books for the descriptions of coitus. I want to make everybody happy. This, as always, is my primary objective.

Now then. Imagine a primal scene. Any primal scene will do . . .

CHAPTER 43

In lieu of a primal scene, I give you the subject of a recent email I received from a friendly Nigerian:

SHE LIKES IT BIGGER AND LONGER

CHAPTER 44

My wife and I take our kids to the zoo every Saturday. Last Saturday her sister came with us. She's a pharmacist.

We went to the Lion's Den.

"That's a tiger," said my sister-in-law.

"There aren't any stripes on it," said my wife.

"Yeah, I know," said my sister-in-law, "but there's no mane either."

My older daughter said, "You know, zebras have stripes. There are stripes all over zebras."

My younger daughter said, "Yeah, I know, but they're still horses."

"They're not horses, they're zebras," said my older daughter. "Horses are horses."

"I know horses are horses," said my sister-in-law, "but that's a tiger . . ."

CHAPTER 45

Do you want to see somebody get excited? Tell a meteorologist there's a tornado down the street. Even better, tell the meteorologist you're not sure if there's a tornado down the street. To optimize a reaction, tell the meteorologist that, down the street, a lot of people are screaming and going crazy as a result of weather-related conditions. You'll never see such an outpouring of enthusiasm. Even diehard futball fans don't get that riled up, and they mean business.

Nobody cares about you.

I'm serious.

It doesn't matter what you do. Kill an insect or kill a god. Everybody is either too stupid and ignorant and

apathetic or too busy going through their motions. Usually all of it.

A menacing thundercloud rolls across the sky like an avalanche of meaning. Its retractable funnel never makes an appearance and remains firmly locked in the cloaca, disappointing thousands of onlookers.

Here's a great idea for a novel, or a screenplay, or a daydream, or whatever. It's guaranteed to make you money. I should charge you for this idea but you paid for *Freud: The Penultimate Biography* and I assume you paid for *Hitler: The Terminal Biography* too. That's good enough. So here's the idea:

Come up with a bunch of characters from disparate social backgrounds and intersect their relationships!

"Donepezil," somebody says, lightheaded.

My lungs hurt from smoking too much.

The real problem is that I don't smoke enough.

I'll smoke a pack, like, every three or four days, in one evening, nursing it with a pint of liquor. It'd be better if I smoked one or two packs per day all day long. My body would be used to the steady injections of nicotine, and it wouldn't have to endure several days of skin-crawling detox once or twice a week, waiting for the next fix.

It takes about 48 hours of clean breathing for your pores to cough the nicotine out of your body.

Once, in college, a fraternity brother dropped a tab of acid into my beer. I tripped for a week, although I remained perfectly functional, going to class, turning in my assignments, etc. I couldn't hear anybody. People would talk to me and their mouths would work in silence. All I could hear were my pores coughing in a symphony

of agony that by week's end had dovetailed into a tolerable spasmodic hum.

Soon I will die of End. I need to change my ways.

One thing I can do is start every new day with a prank call to a car salesman. They deserve to be prank called. And I deserve to be the antagonist on the other end of the line. It's the least I can do for myself.

And finally this quote from Lacan to sand down and smooth out the rough edges of the chapter: "If there is, in fact, something that psychoanalysis has drawn attention to, it is, beyond the sense of obligation properly speaking, the importance, I would even say the omnipresence, of a sense of guilt."

This, then, must be a chronicle of guilt.

CHAPTER 46

Somebody was beating a horse.

"That's a zebra! Look at the stripes! Good lord!" said somebody else.

Sergei Pankejeff couldn't bear it when animals got beaten. It felt like God was beating the crouched vacancy of his soul. He screamed like a woman on the rack.

And entered the horror convention.

Somebody gave him a program and he wandered into the dealer room.

"Wolfman!" said Tom Jésus Savani. The diminutive special effects artist and horror/cult/B-movie actor was sitting behind a fold-out table peddling monster busts and looking angry with his dyed black hair and goatee and all

of the lines that ran down his hard face and his dogged slit of mouth. But he had made a mistake. He thought Pankejeff was Benicio Del Toro, the convention's GOH and star of the film *The Wolfman*.

"My expectations dictate my reality," uttered Pankejeff in a fit of dire mindfulness.

It wasn't the first time he had been mistaken for Benicio Del Toro. It wouldn't be the last. Except for his mustache, they looked almost exactly alike and had the same out-of-shape bodies and smooth off-white skin.

Moments of discomfort passed like gallstones.

Alarmed, Pankejeff checked in to the hotel and went to his room. He turned on the TV, sat on the bed, and thumbed through the program searching for good panels to attend.

GRAND BALLROOM SALON E
10 A.M. Primal Scenes & Doggystyle Sex

GRAND BALLROOM SALON F
11 A.M. White Wolves with Big Tails that Look
More like Foxes or Sheepdogs Sitting in a Tree

LUNCH

GRAND BALLROOM SALON G
1 P.M. How to Eat You Own Hand

GRAND BALLROOM SALON H
2 P.M. How to Murder Your Own Soul

GRAND BALLROOM SALON I
3 P.M. Gay Bestiality & Castration Anxiety

Pankejeff put the program aside. Nothing sounded good. He went to the hospitality suite where they were having a bake sale. He pretended to be interested only insofar as it got him closer to the beverage table. There was no vodka, but gin flowed in abundance, and gin was the same color as vodka and more or less had the same effects on him. He got drunk and ended up talking to Tom Jésus Savani, who ignored him, reserving his conversational energy for Benicio Del Toro.

Benicio Del Toro never showed up to the hospitality suite. And he didn't show up to the convention until Sunday evening after everybody had gone home.

CHAPTER 47

My publisher has been taking it much easier on me now that I'm writing about Freud instead of Hitler notwithstanding how well *Hitler: The Terminal Biography* has done. You can't believe how many copies sold last week alone. More than the other books I've written combined, and one of those bought me a condo on the Italian Riviera. I can't blame my publisher for having reservations about using Hitler—his image on the cover of *Hitler: The Terminal Biography*, I mean; covers are what sell books, and the first sentences of books—to make money, but it's not like there's going to be a lawsuit. They bought the rights to the image and we can do whatever we want with it. Same with the image of Freud on the cover of *Freud: The Penultimate Biography*, but again,

people are less interested in the father of psychoanalysis than the Führer of the Third Reich, and I suspect that this book won't sell anywhere near as many copies. Maybe it will. Trilogies tend to snowball regardless of how good or bad their covers and their first sentences are, and both titles have already been optioned for films. Also, I have been giving the editor-in-chief a lot of backrubs lately. Everybody involved with the publisher is usually quite happy as long as the editor-in-chief gets regular massages. Unfortunately I live in a different state and have to fly out whenever her back really needs attention. She claims that knots gravitate to her scapula region like mosquitoes to a bag of blood, and she says things like, "I have so many knots in my back I should sell them on eBay." For the record, knots are a myth perpetuated by people who want their backs rubbed and by chiropractors and masseuses who need more clients. THEY DO NOT EXIST. A muscle doesn't twist up like a shoelace. I try to explain this to the editor-in-chief, and I tell her that she doesn't have to rely on the pretense of "knots"—I'll come and rub her back anyway as long as the liquor cabinet is at full capacity and she sends out the copyeditor to buy me cigarettes when I run out. But she insists on the "knots," so we mostly just keep quiet about it now.

CHAPTER 48

I received my Ph.D. in How to Tell the Truth from
Zinfandel University in Switzerland. There are hardly any
African Americans in Switzerland and there is accord-
ingly no racism and they even took down the stoplights
after awhile and nobody got in an accident. It was as
close to Utopia as I've ever gotten despite the irritant of
my dissertation committee who, except for my advisor,
didn't like what I ended up writing on and wanted to fail
me. Two of them refused to endorse the final product. At
my dissertation defense, one of them urged me to revise
the final product before submitting it to the University
Protectorate. He wanted me to focus more on the role of
the city and urban space within the context of Honesty

and Rectitude. I said ok and didn't revise it. I said thanks to the committee members who rejected me and shook their hands. My advisor had the final say-so. He passed my dissertation and I received my Ph.D. in How to Tell the Truth from Zinfandel University in Switzerland.

CHAPTER 49

Danny Schreber learned how to dance by watching the American musical variety show *Soul Train*.

Every day his mother went to work, his sisters went to their friends' houses, and he stayed home and watched *Soul Train*, practicing his moves.

He got pretty good and one day somebody kidnapped him because they were watching him through the window and thought to themselves man that boy can dance all right. Danny had always worried about being kidnapped and never wanted to see his face on a milk carton but now he'd be on every milk carton in the state and he'd never taken a good picture in his whole life what with his face and hair and everything.

By the time they got back to the kidnapper's house, Danny was extremely depressed and kind of paranoid and hysterical. But once he got out of the van he felt a little better breathing in the fresh air and then the kidnapper introduced him to the family as "The Dancing Boy" and they ate dinner. Salisbury steak and macaroni and cheese. No vegetables.

"All right now dance boy dance," said the kidnapper after dinner and everybody looked on. But Danny was scared and anyway he realized that he couldn't really dance without the TV on. Everybody was riotously unhappy and there were some harsh words and invective but soon the kidnapper threw up his hands and said something like ok fine whatever and drove him home and told him to grow up and get lost. Danny thanked him and was so relieved that nobody would get to see some goofy picture of him on a damn milk carton.

He never watched *Soul Train* again.

CHAPTER 50

Danny Schreber was watching *Soul Train* again and somebody rang the doorbell. Who could that be in the middle of the day? Danny thought to himself but he didn't get the door. The bell kept ringing and ringing and ringing, though, and eventually he got mad and turned off the TV and went to the door and got on a stool and looked through the peephole.

It was his father.

"Dad what the heck're ya doing out there? Shouldn't you be at work?" said Danny.

"Open up son. I've come home early," said his father.

"Dad I don't know how I feel about that. It seems weird. You've never come home in the middle of the day before."

"Open up son."

"Dad I don't know if I can. I'm scared."

"Son now you open up this door now. I'm not gonna ask you again now."

"Don't you have a key though? You, like, own the house and stuff."

"Oh yeah that's right." Danny's father put the key in the door and turned it and turned it and turned it. He couldn't get it to work. "It's not working," he said.

"Here Dad let me try to open it from the inside." Danny turned the lock but the door wouldn't open. He turned the knob but the door wouldn't open. He tried the lock again and then the knob again and still nothing worked. "Nothing's working Dad. We're stuck on either side of this here door."

"Don't get hyper son. Here let me try something." He took a few steps backward and rammed the door with his shoulder. He did it again. He kept ramming it until his shoulder started to hurt. "Jesus Christ this fuckin' door!" He rammed it one more time and apologized for swearing. Then he told Danny to back up a little because he was going to get an axe and by God he'd chop that door all the way down to the ground if he had to. He left and Danny waited and waited and waited and waited and waited and waited and waited but his father never came back. So he returned to the kitchen and turned on the TV.

He never saw his father again.

CHAPTER 51

Danny Schreber was playing ball with his father again. They played ball together almost every day.

"Hey Dad do you think I'll grow up to be the first person who lives forever?" asked Danny.

His father said something but the wind was blowing too loud and Danny didn't hear him.

They continued to play ball and Danny grew up to be a distinguished yet psychotic judge. Among the delusions that plagued him was the belief that God intended to turn him into a woman via the coerced retreat of his penis into his body in an effort to form a vagina. According to Danny in *Memoirs of My Nervous Illness*, a record of the architecture of his madness:

Twice at different times . . . I had a female genital organ, although a poorly developed one, and in my body felt quickening like the first signs of life of a human embryo: by a divine miracle God's nerves corresponding to male seed had been thrown into my body; in other words fertilization had occurred.

Adulthood can sting like a wasp. If only boys didn't have to become men. This is not a joke. Sigmund Freud diagnosed Schreber as a latent homosexual with repressed feelings for his father. He never met Schreber. But he read his memoirs, and that seemed like enough information to go on.

Stop.

CHAPTER 52

These characters are getting out of control. Who do we have so far?

Danny Schreber.

Freud.

The mechanic.

Dick Cavett.

Donovan Ogg.

Benicio Del Toro.

Tom Jésus Savani

Sergei Whatshisname.

Zebras.

Anybody else? I'm sure there's somebody else. You. And you.

Everybody's better off if I only have to keep track of one or two people. Preferably one.

What would a mechanic do in this situation?

Regroup. Reconnoiter. Reread.

A conclusion is immanent. Somehow garlic baloney make sense. *Freud: The Penultimate Biography* possesses able-bodied flatfeet. Sleights-of-hand are only as good as the curvature of the lifeline in the palm.

CHAPTER 53

Readers of *Hitler: The Terminal Biography* may notice that my publisher is virtually nonexistent in *Freud: The Penultimate Biography*. So is my wife. The reason has to do with my subject matter: this is not a biography of Adolf Hitler, but Sigmund Freud. With the exception of several requests to fly out and take care of the yard and the house, I have heard nothing from my publisher, and my wife has started ignoring me again. Unlike my initial experience writing *Hitler: The Terminal Biography*, I'm having no difficulty whatsoever propelling this narrative forward like a flaming hippopotamus corpse launched from a capable trebuchet, but you need to read the Hitler book to sort of get what I'm doing. I have also been using Freud as a focal register

far more regularly than I used Hitler. I guess Freud's more interesting (although somehow less compelling). But what matters is that you will be able to understand what I'm doing, why I'm doing it, where I'm going, and why I'm going there. There it is and here we are.

CHAPTER 54

Return of the Living Dead Part II just came on HBO. 0% of critics on the tomatometer liked it. Is this the one where the red-haired goth-girl gets naked and dances on top of the gravestone like a holy pariah? That might have been in the first one. Or the third one.

Originally I intended to feature characters from Freud's major case studies in this biography. The case studies include "From the History of an Infantile Neurosis" (Wolfman), "Notes upon a Case of Obsessional Neurosis" (Ratman), "Psychoanalytic Notes Upon an Autobiographical Account of a Case of Paranoia" (Schreber), and "Dora: An Analysis of a Case of Hysteria" (some girl). Wolfman and Schreber are the only ones that made it in. I could try to do something

with the Ratman and Dora but honestly I'm running out of room and steam. I've given myself a maximum count of 15,000 words and I intend to stick that number in the lawn. It's a good number. It's a gift. Nobody wants to read more than 15,000 words in one book.

This zombie movie isn't very good. I can't tell if it's supposed to be serious or not.

I'm not going to ask the publisher to increase the font or the margins in this biography so that the final product looks longer than it actually is. They didn't end up widening the margins in *Hitler: The Terminal Biography* in spite of my requests, but they jacked up the font, and together with all of those short chapters that each received their own page (not to mention that every chapter started halfway down the page)—that was enough to get over 140 pages in total.

I'm really drunk now but I'm pretty lucid and functional too. I rarely drink to the point of dysfunction. But I definitely have a problem.

There must be another movie on. The more I look the less there is.

I should go to less writing conventions. I went to at least 20 last year. That's too many, especially considering that I never have a good time, that I always have big expectations on Friday and subzero spirits on Sunday. Nearly half of the Sundays last year, then, I was upset, depressed, consternated, remorseful and misanthropic.

Only Mother truly cares.

And Ego.

There's always breakfast, Nespresso, and the clarity of simple mornings.

I never smoke cigarettes before 5 p.m. Cigarettes and nicotine in general can be useful for bodybuilding when you're dieting for a competition and get food cravings.

I can't remember when the next competition is.

Where did I put the remote.

There it is.

It's not working. The batteries are dead.

Veins.

Nerves.

Out the window, a human tendril reaches across the yellow moon and conjures an imaginary disaster.

I'm going to write one more paragraph after this one and finish the chapter. The paragraph will contain good advice and an element of truth. Don't be deceived by its ostensible nonchalance.

Somebody closes the window.

CHAPTER 55

Donovan Ogg, in addition to being a movie director—is a bodybuilder.

Not just by self-definition. Ogg won Mr. Europe, Mr. Universe and Mr. Olympia and he's shredded from neck to ankles. I can't rightly tear through this biography without dispensing some bodybuilding advice. Again, the mind is the prison of the body and vice versa. There's no breaking out of the prison, but inescapable periods of incarceration necessitate noir-like grit.

In *Hitler: The Terminal Biography*, I concentrated on workouts. Now I want to talk about diet. Generally I eat about 6-8 small meals a day, unless I get drunk at night, in which case I only eat 2-3 small meals amounting to no

more than 1000 calories, since I drink about 1500 to 2000 calories in alcohol. Here's what I ate yesterday. I didn't drink any alcohol.

MEAL #1
1 cup egg whites
2 whole eggs
¼ cup raspberries
¼ cup blueberries

MEAL #2 (PRE-WORKOUT)
1 banana
1 tbsp. honey
2.8 oz. solid white albacore tuna

MEAL #3 (POST-WORKOUT)
2 scoops whey protein
1 low-fat Greek yogurt

MEAL #4
1 cup brown rice
1 oz. avocado
4 pieces sashimi tuna
1 cup chopped broccoli

MEAL #5
8 oz. tilapia
1 tbsp. cocktail sauce
4 cups spinach

MEAL #6
2 tbsp. peanut butter
½ cup skim milk

MEAL #7
1 low-fat Greek yogurt
¼ blueberries

MEAL #8
½ cup egg whites
2 whole eggs
3 oz. chicken breast

This might seem like a lot of food, but it only totals about 2200 calories, with approximately 300g of protein, 150g of carbohydrates, and 80g of fat—not enough for a 6'5" 40-year-old male. My protein intake is fine; it should be about 1.5 times my body weight and I weigh 200 lbs., so it's right on the money. My body is completely ripped up— the science fiction author Harlan Ellison once compared me to a hormone-injected beanstalk—but I need to bulk up and put on about twenty more lbs. of lean muscle. This will require jacking up my carb intake with more brown rice and sweet potatoes. I could take care of it with steroids, but they give me acne and when I take steroids all I want to do is maul everybody, especially when I mix them with alcohol. So I keep it clean.

Bear in mind: this is what works for me. Everybody has different metabolisms and needs to figure out what specifically their body needs and how much alcohol they can drink. For instance, my body allows me to get

plastered at least three nights a week, but I suspect others won't be so lucky, or unlucky. Begin by determining how many calories your body needs in order to maintain your current weight. I'd tell you how here but I don't feel like getting online and finding the equation for you so go to www.bodybuilding.com and do it yourself. Once you determine your level of maintenance, add or subtract depending on how much weight you want to lose or gain, but do so by eating WHOLE FOODS ONLY. Absolutely no processed food with the exception of protein powder and the occasional link of organic turkey or chicken sausage.

Finally, shoot for a 40-40-20 macronutritional break-down, i.e., 40% of your calories coming from protein, 40% from carbohydrates, and 20% from fats. I haven't quite figured this out yet but nobody's perfect. You also might find that tweaking your macros (e.g., to 50-30-20, or to 30-50-20) may produce better results in your body than in somebody else's.

Remember that every meal you eat does not and should not involve a hedonism of the taste buds. Perceive food as fuel first. Then seek out different varieties of fuel that best appeal to your tongue and palate.

CHAPTER 56

In the next chapter Donovan Ogg is going to die. Before that, though:

Did you know that Sigmund was a very good basketball player in high school? Not great, mind you. He couldn't dunk very well and he had flat feet, but he could dribble and pass with the best of them and he could bang those boards, blocking out his opponents with mathematical precision. But his greatest strength was all of the trash-talking he did on the court. He never missed an opportunity. An opponent would dribble the ball off of his shoe and he'd say, "Ha! What an innate indication of nervous degeneracy!" An opponent would miss a shot and he'd say, "Ha! Another wish-fulfillment fantasy dries up like a

raisin in the sun!" And when an opponent made a shot: "That ain't nothing but an outburst of homosexual libido!" And, of course, when he'd block somebody's shot, "Get that infantile sexual manifestation outta here!" Coaches didn't like it so much when he tried to run the show, calling out plays they hadn't practiced like "labial zone offenses" and "full cathexis presses," but they tolerated him in light of his team spirit.

Following a knee injury that required orthoscopic surgery, Sigmund opted to give up basketball and focus on other pursuits.

CHAPTER 57

According to the news, Donovan Ogg was found dead at the bottom of a swimming people.

They say he had been drinking and smoking marijuana all night long prior to the incident.

Apparently his wife woke up around 2 a.m. and heard him yelling and screaming out in the backyard. Mrs. Ogg went downstairs and saw her naked husband outside storming across the grass and pounding on the sliding glass doors yelling for her to open up. She got scared and went back upstairs and thought about what to do for awhile and accidentally fell back asleep because earlier she had doubled up on Ambien.

Around 5 a.m., reports confirm that Mrs. Ogg was

awoken again by a great splash. She got out of bed and hurried downstairs and smashed through the sliding glass doors into the backyard where Donovan Ogg lay dead at the bottom of the pool.

Somebody had drained the pool but moisture was still readily apparent on the pool walls and especially on Ogg's glistening body.

Forensics experts showed up instantly, as if expecting the tragedy.

They determined that Ogg had smoked at least an ounce of marijuana earlier in the evening in conjunction with drinking a skull of Crystal Head vodka and possibly a bottle of Kim Crawford sauvignon blanc. There was no nicotine in his system and nothing stronger than weed and alcohol.

Local law enforcement officers initially ruled the famous director's death a suicide, but the matter is being reconsidered in light of his erratic behavior earlier in the evening, which was, according to his wife and close friends, in "dire contrast" to his usual character. This may have included a high-speed car chase the day before, but the perpetrator got away, and while Ogg's car had been identified as the car in question, there was no way to determine if Ogg had been behind the wheel.

Coroner officials say everybody's questions will be answered in the wake of an autopsy, but it will take up to two months to process toxicology, DNA, and post-cognitive tests. Thanks to a neighbor's penchant for tape recording the sound of night crickets, however, we have relatively static-free footage of Ogg's last word prior to him falling (or being thrown into) the pool:

"Wolfman!"

Curiously, Ogg's final will and testament was found crumpled into a ball on a patio chair near the pool. It is said that the late director's wife was disappointed to discover that he left nothing to her or their kids but rather made a request for all of his property, assets and monies to be delivered to the moon.

Arrangements are currently underway to ensure that his desires, as inscribed onto papyrus, are fulfilled.

CHAPTER 58

A dead man lies in the blue grave.

Gleaming, I look down and say, "Well at least he doesn't have to shave anymore. Shaving's one of the biggest pains in the world. Every morning and so forth. Jesus. And do you know how expensive razors are? I spent, like, eleven dollars the other day on five blades. Five blades! That's depressing. Seriously."

Somebody says a prayer and then I get in my Mini Cooper and drive away.

CHAPTER 59

Freud's concept of the death drive was riotously contro-
versial and divisive. First proffered in *Beyond the Pleasure
Principle*, it made him something of a laughingstock
among his disciples and other psychoanalysts when they
talked about it in the beer halls. Still, Freud held fast to
the concept of the death drive until the day he died. Years
later Lacan picked up the ball and situated the death drive
within the symbolic order, not the imaginary order, where
it technically belonged. His point was that the death drive
is merely a symptom of the predisposition in the symbolic
order to generate repetition. On the subject of repetition,
Dylan Evans, author of *An Introductory Dictionary of
Lacanian Psychoanalysis*, probably the most enjoyable

book I've read in years, maybe ever, an unbridled and unmitigated page-turner (I'm not kidding), has this to say:

> Freud's most important discussion of the repetition compulsion (*Weiderholungszwang*) occurs in *Beyond the Pleasure Principle* where he links it to the concept of the death drive. Freud posited the existence of a basic compulsion to repeat in order to explain certain clinical data: namely, the tendency of the subject to expose himself again and again to distressing situations. It is a basic principle of psychoanalysis that a person is only condemned to repeat something when he has forgotten the origins of the compulsion, and that psychoanalytic treatment can therefore break the cycle of repetition by helping the patient remember.

CHAPTER 60

To be among the Embryonic.

In anticipation of the bog and the colorful sulfur pools out of which bubble the same asymptomatic Stink . . .

Freud: The Penultimate Biography will go down in history as a book that went down in history.

"Not recommended for traditional readers."

CHAPTER 61

A dead man climbs out of the blue grave. Everybody gets nervous but eventually they grow accustomed to what happened and in time they forget about the dead man altogether. I'm not there. I'm at Walgreens, Mini Cooper idling in the parking lot. I'm complaining about the price of razorblades to the cashier. She doesn't know why I blame her but somebody needs to be held accountable.

CHAPTER 62

They say that everybody is entitled to an opinion, but in the human experience, such an ideological free-for-all has led to immeasurable traumas, ranging from the smallest neuroses to the deadliest wars. I have only tried to write something as fast as I possibly can so that you will understand it. I know everybody's interested in understanding what they read and what I write.

CHAPTER 63

Here's a tip: the more you critique this book, the more it will critique you.

Freud: The Penultimate Biography is an anvil of play-back—much stronger than your pong.

There's only room on this flying island for one exegete.

A prescribed devotion to the gongs of violence and the gods of terminal construction inevitably backslides into an ataxia of Names and Numbers.

Like the Therapist, I know what you're going to say before you say it, before you even know you're going to say it. You wear your massification on your faceplate.

My intention is to save you from the *mobile vulgus.*

Bande de moebius. The children of metonymy.

Mother!

If nothing else, please holster your inhibitions for a moment so that you can learn something about the Father of psychoanalysis.

He is a meaningful figure.

Nobody in recorded history compares to him.

Red-rimmed insecurities obstruct justice. Aspire to appreciate *Freud: The Penultimate Biography* for what it really is: a treatise on a man who wanted to help people while carving out his own legacy.

This double-edged endeavor is made even nobler by its very identity as a conflation of aggressive Ego and rawhide Altruism.

You don't need to read the book. Buying it is enough. I promise you will enjoy running your fingertips up and down the soft matte cover, which feels a like dehydrated rubber cement.

Resistance is permissible, although my ekphrasis will inevitably transcend your angle of resignation.

And your qualms, like my clarity, will soon lapse into the womb of oblivion.

CHAPTER 64

Coming soon: *Douglass: The Lost Autobiography*. We'll begin on a slave plantation floating across outer space in a containment bubble à la Jonathan Swift's Laputa. Frederick Douglass has been hiding out in a shed for weeks with nothing but a pair of kettlebells, ample supplies of anabolic steroids, eight skulls of Crystal Head vodka, and several advanced reader copies of *Hitler: The Terminal Biography* and *Freud: The Penultimate Biography*, studying his craft and preparing to "discuss the terms of his freedom" with the Master of Ceremonies and Guest of Honor . . .

FREUD

THE PENULTIMATE BIOGRAPHY

ABOUT THE AUTHOR

D. HARLAN WILSON is an award-winning, critically acclaimed novelist, short story writer, theorist, editor, historian, publisher and English professor. Visit him online at **DHarlanWilson.com** and **TheKyotoMan.com**.

An icon of true evil, Adolf Hitler is arguably the most important figure of the twentieth century. No one has so patently demonstrated the horrific capabilities of mankind. In *Hitler: The Terminal Biography*, D. Harlan Wilson tracks the life of the infamous monomaniac from struggling artist to mass murderer. Based on more than ten years of archival research and German sociological study, this one-volume account covers ground previously uncharted by other biographers, drawing heavily on newfound diaries, letters, and phonograph recordings of Hitler's closest confidants as well as the Führer himself.

"An extraordinary and masterful work. Wilson has written the biography to end all biographies." **GIDEON JOHNSON PILLOW**, Professor of History and Chair of African-American Studies at the University of Fostoria

www.RawDogScreaming.com

Frederick Douglass stands as one of American history's most extraordinary figures, overcoming the evils of slavery and racial construction by force of will and grit. As a fervent abolitionist, gifted orator, and sagacious editor and author, he became one of the most outspoken and influential social reformers of his time. During his life, he published three autobiographies chronicling his struggle from childhood to adulthood, from slave to free man, from ignorance to power-knowledge. And yet the full narrative of the life of Frederick Douglass, contrary to popular belief, has been incomplete . . . until now. Recently recovered on an archeological dig in Ireland, where Douglass lectured extensively in the 1840s, this heretofore "lost" autobiography marks the fourth and final work in the library of his selfhood. Tying together loose ends in the previous three autobiographies while exposing remarkable, often disturbing secrets about his private life, Douglass portrays himself not only as a man of words and character but as a kind of anachronistic hipster and proto-beatnik. There is a reason this volume never saw publication during his lifetime. A reason—and a method.

"Once again, D. Harlan Wilson biographizes with a hammer. Beware." **WILLIAM CLARKE QUANTRILL**, Professor of Religious Studies and Director of the Booker T. Washington Institute for African and African-American Research at the University of Fostoria

www.RawDogScreaming.com